MAY THE FORCE BE WITH YOU

From Luke Walker

January 30, 1991

VIKING

Published by the Penguin Group
Penguin Books Ltd, 27 Wrights Lane, London W8 5TZ, England
Penguin Books USA Inc., 375 Hudson Street, New York, New York 10014, USA
Penguin Books Australia Ltd, Ringwood, Victoria, Australia
Penguin Books Canada Ltd, 10 Alcorn Avenue, Toronto, Ontario, Canada M4V 3B2
Penguin Books (NZ) Ltd, 182-190 Wairau Road, Auckland 10, New Zealand

Penguin Books Ltd, Registered Offices: Harmondsworth, Middlesex, England

First published 1994
1 3 5 7 9 10 8 6 4 2
First edition

Filmset in Sabon

Made and printed in Belgium

A CIP catalogue record for this book is available from the British Library

ISBN 0-670-85062-4

ARIA

Written by
PETER ELBLING

Illustrated by
SOPHY WILLIAMS

VIKING

WHAT made Aria different from her brothers and sisters was not that she was the youngest or the prettiest, but that she could not speak.

"Arrr, arrr," Aria said, making a rasping noise in the back of her throat.

Aria spent her days playing in the jungle, far away from the taunts of the village children. There she imitated the parrots, macaws and other multi-coloured birds of the wild.

"AWK, AWK," she called to the toucan.

"Braak, braak," she cawed as they built their nests.

Soon the birds became used to Aria and returned her rasps with squawks of their own. "Cheep, cheep. DeJip, DeJip."

The jungle rang with their conversation.

ARIA'S joy was complete. She watched the birds feed their young, listened to their songs of love and dreamed of gliding through the air with their grace and ease.

But because Aria was afraid the men of the village might catch the birds and sell them in the marketplace, she kept her secret behind her smile.

"WHAT'S she got to be so happy about?" said a birdseller to his companion. "She can't talk, she doesn't have any money and she spends all day in the jungle."

"Tomorrow, let's follow her and find out," said the other.

The next morning the two men squeezed through bushes and climbed over trees until at last they came to a small clearing. There they watched in amazement as birds of all sizes and species chirped with Aria like village women gossiping over a pot of maize.

"Let's get away from here," said the birdseller's companion. "This girl is crazy."

"I HAVE a better idea," said the birdseller, and he raced from his hiding-place and grabbed a beautiful red Cardinal that was sitting on Aria's shoulder.

"We'll get plenty of money for this one," he shouted.

"Arck, arck," screamed the Cardinal.

"Arr, arr," pleaded Aria.

"What did she say?" asked the other man.

"Who cares," laughed the bird-seller. "Let's go to market."

Aria sank to the ground and wept.

ARIA did not want to stay in the village any longer. Nothing her brothers or sisters could say would change her mind. So after kissing them goodbye, she set off on her own.

SHE wandered through the jungle calling to her friends, but they flew away and screeched at her from the safety of the tree-tops.

"Jeee, jeee, jeee, jeee, jeee, jeee, jeee."

That night she built a bed in the lower branches of a jacaranda tree and rocked herself to sleep by the light of the moon.

FROM watching the birds, Aria learned how to take care of herself.

The blue berries are good, but the white ones are bitter, she thought. Like the birds, she washed in the waterfalls and played in the clear, fresh pools.

EVERY day, she gathered feathers from the jungle floor. Deep red plumes the colour of her dreams, lavender tufts no bigger than her fingers, fluffy white crests softer than her breath.

"I will weave them into a cloak and wear it about my shoulders," she smiled, "to remind me of my friends."

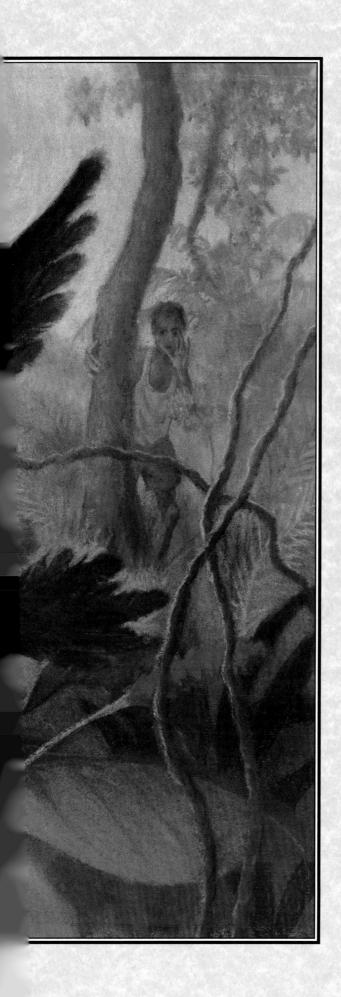

BUT Aria's greatest pleasure came whenever she spied a birdseller trying to catch a bird by imitating its call.

"Dejip, Dejip," she warned the Guan.

"Dejip, Dejip," the Guan piped gratefully as it flew off into the trees.

NOT long after, Aria was dancing in a shaft of sunlight when the jungle screamed with danger. Peering through the thick, green foliage, she saw a band of angry men coming towards her.

"You scared away our birds," shouted the birdseller. "You must pay us back."

Aria threw her feather cape about her shoulders and sped away. At first she eluded the men easily, laughing at their clumsiness. But they were determined.

"You won't escape," they cried. "We will catch you."

They forced Aria deeper and deeper into the bush. She could hear their footsteps, feel their desire for revenge. Exhausted, she stumbled on until she came to the edge of a cliff.

THE men poured out of the jungle behind her. "There she is," they cried.

Aria was trapped. Suddenly, the sky above her filled with birds. All the birds she had ever known. Aria raised her arms. The cape billowed behind her, its colours shimmering in the midday heat.

"Arrr, arrr," Aria called.

"Jeep, jeep, cawww, cawww, DeJip, DeJip," the birds called back.

Aria closed her eyes and jumped.

FOR a moment, Aria felt herself falling. Then a great rush of wind carried her forward. She opened her eyes. The tree-tops were speeding by beneath her. She looked to either side and her eyes filled with wonder. The birds were sweeping, soaring, sailing her into the blue beyond.

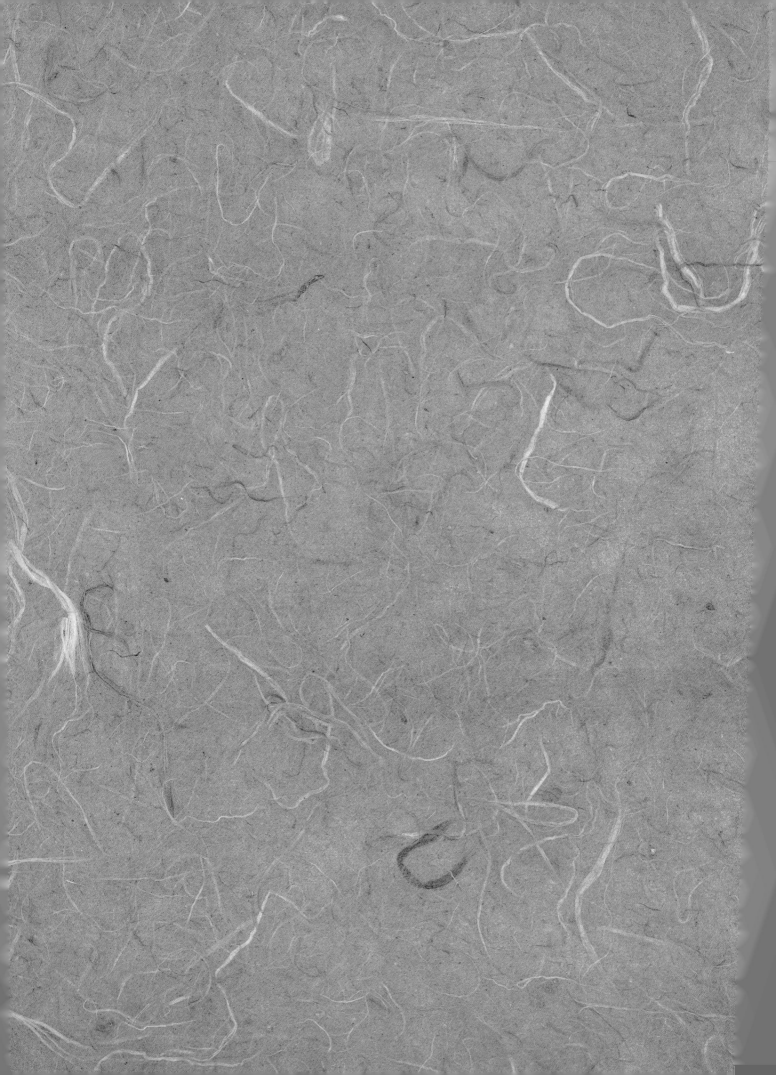